Messages from the Breathless

WINNER OF THE BOOKLOGIX 2011

YOUNG *Writers* CONTEST

To Didi ♡
Keep Reading!

—Sam McLeod

Messages

From the
Breathless

Messages

FROM THE
BREATHLESS

Savannah McLeod

BOOKLOGIX®
Alpharetta, GA

Copyright © 2012 Savannah McLeod

All Rights Reserved. No part of this book may be reproduced, scanned, or distributed in any printed or electronic form without written permission from Savannah McLeod.

ISBN 978-1-61005-135-4

Library of Congress Control Number: 2012904054

Printed in the United States of America

This paper meets the requirements of ANSI/NISO Z39.48-1992 (Permanence of Paper)

Aéropostale® is a registered trademark of Aeropostale, Inc.
iPod® is a registrered trademark of Apple Inc.
Facebook® is a registered trademark of Facebook, Inc.
Vera Bradley® is a registered trademark of Vera Bradley Designs, Inc.

Messages from the Breathless is a work of fiction. Names, places, and incidents are either products of the author's imagination or are used fictitiously. Any resemblances of the fictional characters and events to actual people and events are coincidental.

TABLE OF CONTENTS

Acknowledgements	ix
Chapter 1: Messages from the Breathless	1
Chapter 2: Disappearing Evidence	23
Chapter 3: Discovering Lies	33
Chapter 4: Gold with Black Calligraphy	65
Afterword	73

ACKNOWLEDGEMENTS

Messages from the Breathless would not have been possible without the help of many others. I would like to thank Ahmad, Angela, and Sara from BookLogix for making this book possible. I would also like to thank Sundra Paul from Ananchel Photography for taking the cover photos which included Sarah Freet, Blake Leavy, Parker McLeod, and Kyle McLaren. The help from my friends and family have made this experience so much more enjoyable.

CHAPTER 1

MESSAGES FROM THE BREATHLESS

My breath turned foggy white every time I exhaled—it was cold. The clouds were a melancholy gray; they looked as if they formed a somber, cotton blanket covering the sleeping sky. The morning seemed as if it had not woken. My mind went blank. It had only been three weeks since Hunter had passed away, and I knew I still loved him.

It was troubling to think about how he and his father had been in a car crash, especially with just the two of them sitting in the tiny car without seatbelts. I knew he was a Christian, just like I was, and he was in a wonderful place spending time with Jesus. I knew that the time until I would greet him again would seem to be everlasting. Although I missed hearing his laugh, I was confident that I would find someone just as humorous and brilliant as he was…eventually. I thought about how shy I'd become after his death.

Suddenly, an arctic wind swept my straight, elbow-length, blonde hair into a rat's nest. My hair was blowing in every direction, seeming as if it was shivering in sync with my body. I crossed my arms, struggling to stay warm as I inched my way to the bus stop.

"Hey! Alicia, do you have the homework from last night? I forgot to study for the vocabulary test!" Catherine's agitating voice rang in my ears. I remember when I used to actually like her and not just pretend. I used to look up to her, but then she started trying to be just like me and telling me that my life was perfect. She started following me, and now, every time I turn around in the halls of my high school, she is always right there. She used to like Hunter, too. She never admitted it, but it was obvious. How could she say my life was perfect after someone I was close to is now gone?

I never replied to Catherine's question. I was in my own world, oblivious to everything. The bus pulled up and I sat in seat five with Catherine next to me. I began to gaze out the window like most tiring mornings. I thought about Hunter's funeral. He was buried with everything that had been found with him the day he died, along with flowers and gifts placed around his tombstone. When he was found dead that gruesome day, he had his phone in his pocket. It was buried with him. That's what everyone I knew had told me. I would never forget what his phone looked like—it was unlike anyone else's. The case was a shiny golden color and "Hunter" was written on it in black bold calligraphy letters. Now, it was almost too much to even see his name in my contact list. I had considered deleting it, but decided not to as a memory of him. I remembered how whenever he would text me, my favorite song would play. Soon after he died I changed that song to "Wordless Goodbye," by one of my favorite singers,

Kara Keathly. I knew I would never hear that song play on my phone ever again.

"Alicia, we're here." Catherine's voice prompted me to get out of my seat, where I had been sitting in a daze. I stepped off the bus, with Catherine following closely behind me. The noise of my silver sandals clicking against the concrete sounded like rain banging on the roads. I walked into school and several people turned and glanced at me. Everyone in the entire high school knew that I had been going out with Hunter. A couple of my friends would usually come talk to me before each of my classes, but they all hated Catherine and noticed that she followed me. They didn't want to be with her at all, even if it meant not being with me.

I walked down the halls trying to look confident—but I knew I wasn't. I opened my locker to grab my binders for homeroom. Shortly after that, I headed to science class and took a seat. I must have forgotten to set my phone to silent.

"*You left, without saying a word. And now, you're hidden from the world,*" began sounding from my phone. Oh No!

"Alicia Flynn! Are you texting during class?"

"No, sir! I meant to leave my phone in my locker. I'm so sorry," I answered. His crystal-blue eyes seemed as if they could do something fatal to me with just a single glare. I looked down, ashamed. Suddenly, he turned away and continued teaching. I began singing the song that had played in my head. Wait, I recognized that song! It was "Wordless Goodbye"! But—that's impossible! Isn't it? Hunter's phone was buried with him! Even if some miracle had happened and he was still alive, his phone would never get a signal several feet underground. Would it? My palms began to itch; I was yearning to check my phone for texts. What if he really was texting me? Is that so impossible? I knew I had heard that song!

The bell sounded and my heart thudded. Students swarmed from every direction like they were speeding automobiles hustling to the finish line. I advanced into the hallway to find Jenny waiting for me outside of my class. Jenny was my best friend.

"Sorry, I have to get going right now. There is something I have to do," I told her.

"Okay, then! See you later!" she replied, vivaciously strolling down the hall. Her ostentatious, glittering navy blue necklace clicked against her neck with every couple steps she took. I hurried to my locker to check my phone. I couldn't believe it; had Hunter honestly texted me? I rummaged through my inky-black purse searching for my phone. Once I had a hold of it, I leaned against my locker and began to slide it open.

One new message from Hunter

Thump! I swear I heard my heart beating against my chest! I clicked *view*, and then held my breath—afraid of what might happen next. I rubbed my eyes as I saw the screen. It was impossibly surreal. It read:

Hey, it's Hunter. It's so pitch-black down here. I wouldn't even be able to see without the light of my phone.

I was in shock. Is he still alive? Even if he had been buried alive, he would have suffocated by now! I quickly pressed my fingers against multiple buttons typing a message in return.

Are you okay? Are you still alive? How are you texting me? I know they buried you with the phone, but this is impossible! How in the world are you texting me? –Alicia

I was shaken, as if I was a skyscraper that had been toppled and ripped apart by a massive tsunami. I made my way to my next class, and before I knew it, school was over. I found my way to the bus, listening to Catherine go on and on and on with the most boring story.

"You've been so silent today. Everything okay?" Catherine questioned, her curly brown hair fell down past her shoulders, and her glistening green eyes were locked on mine. I knew everyone was aware that the reason I was being so doleful was because of

Hunter's death. Yet, no one seemed to mention it to me.

"I'm fine. Just exhausted," I mumbled as I glanced down at my nails, trying to evade her curious stare. The entire bus ride home I was re-thinking the day. The message I had received made me paranoid. The bus came to a halt, and Catherine and I stepped onto the grass.

"Can you hang out today?" she asked, her head tilted to the side. I shook my head no. I had much more important things to do than to worry about her. I sprinted home, sick of being around Catherine, and ready to be alone to solve my own problems. My fists clenched. I was afraid. I was deeply afraid of what Hunter's response would be. If there ever was one.

"You left, without saying a word. And now, you're hidden from the world."

My breath skidded. My head felt heavy on my shoulders. I jumped up the brick steps at the foot of my house and opened the cream-colored door.

"You okay? How was school today?" my dad asked on his way outside to the grill.

"Fine I guess. I have to start my homework," I announced as I scampered up the carpeted steps to my bedroom and locked the door shut. I gulped, bringing my fingers through my silky hair. I undid the clasp on my silver bracelet as the symphonic noise of metal charms banging against each other sounded. I placed it in my dresser drawer and slowly slid my phone open. Before I even saw the message, the rain clouds inside of my mind released water onto my skin. Mascara began spreading across my face, but that didn't matter at all. I began to read the message, whispering the words to myself as if reading them in my head wasn't enough.

The end is not the end. It's the very beginning.

I couldn't believe what I saw. How could he be saying this? I was glad he was optimistic; I assumed that he was trying to tell me he was in Heaven. I smiled. The tears in my eyes flowed stronger, but I was delighted to know he was in a better place. I knew he was resting in peace, and decided I wouldn't message him back tonight. It would take me a while to imagine what things would be worth messaging to Hunter. What could be worth messaging to the breathless?

"Alicia! Dinner time!" my mother called. I scurried down the steps to my seat in the kitchen. My parents and I joined hands to say a blessing. My plate was topped with a steaming, juicy hamburger, and a glass full of smooth, white milk accompanied it.

"How was your day?" my mother asked me, passing the ketchup to my father.

"It was fine. Hunter was buried with his phone, right?" I whispered in response. My parents exchanged concerned glances as if they had hoped to skip discussing Hunter's death during mealtime.

"That's what we heard. Why do you ask?" My parents just looked at me. They were curious.

"Just wondering." The rest of dinner we ate silently. My heart ached to spill everything that had happened between Hunter and me that day. It was best if I waited until a better time to have a conversation about the messages. I carried my plate to the sink, and began working on my homework. Before I got into bed I checked my Facebook. I had a couple notifications. I finished checking them, and began to scroll down the news feed when suddenly my mouth dropped. Hunter had updated his status twenty-three minutes ago! I bet others could see it too. The white "M" surrounded by a black circle marked the bottom of the status; it stood for mobile. Obviously, he had accessed Facebook using his cell phone. My eyes raced back and forth to read his status:

Thanks everyone for caring about me and my father and posting on my wall. Especially Alicia.

I gulped, was this true? Could others see this?! I knew my parents were friends with him on Facebook! They could probably see the post too! I rushed downstairs to my parents who were in the living room.

"Go on Facebook!" I shouted, my silky hair blowing behind me as I hurried to grab the laptop. I handed it to my mother. She laughed.

"Is there some Facebook emergency?" she joked, her fingers jumping from key to key as she typed.

"Go to Hunter's wall!" I ordered, jumping up and down, excited to show her what he had written. She looked at me and then back at the computer. She went to his Facebook page. Nothing there! No new status! Where had it gone? I knew I had seen it!

"Mom, Hunter had just updated his status! I swear! He had been using his phone, from his grave. He was buried with it remember? He had written a status! Why isn't it there anymore?" I asked. I knew they would never believe me now.

"Are you serious?" She glanced at my father and then back at me, a look of utter concern spread across her face.

"I saw it. It was there," I mumbled.

"Honey, we know that you and Hunter were great friends, but there is no way that he could have done that. Are you sure you saw it? Maybe we should go to a counselor," my father said.

"No. He texted me too! I can show you the texts! I'm not psycho!" Without waiting for a response, I scrambled upstairs to get my phone. Once I returned I realized it was dead. I immediately plugged it into a charger.

"Well, it's dead right now, but tomorrow, I will show you the texts! I'm not crazy."

"We never said you were crazy honey. It's sad when people die. Why don't you go to bed?" my mother suggested, smiling.

I crawled into my bed and pulled my blanket over me. I felt trapped in warmth. My scattered thoughts kept me up for a while. How could my parents not believe me? Did Hunter delete his status? I glanced outside the window by my bed hoping for answers. The fiery stars looked like fireworks on the Fourth of July. The moon was a gigantic satellite that clung to the sky.

Glowing and full, it shined upon an old fishing pond near my house. The water seemed to sparkle and dance under the sky—it was beautiful. No matter how much I tried to stop thinking about what my parents said, I couldn't! I knew I wasn't insane! Was I?

CHAPTER 2

DISAPPEARING EVIDENCE

Light filled the inside of my room. My eyes sluggishly opened, and I managed to pull myself out of bed and get dressed. *Ding Dong!* The doorbell rang, and I went downstairs to answer the door. Ugh! It was Catherine.

"Hey! I called your home phone earlier, and your mom said you were still sleeping. She told me that you had nothing to do today and to come by a little bit later. So here I am!" she explained.

"Oh, well okay then," I told her, secretly rolling my eyes as I turned around. Suddenly, the memory of last night hit me like a bullet. I had to show my parents the texts, but now I wouldn't be able to for a while because Catherine was here. I didn't want her to know.

I tried to force my brain to figure something out, but I was out of ideas. Catherine's voice startled me, "Can I see your phone? I think when I entered my number in your contacts I messed up." She smiled; her emerald-green, glistening eyes reminded me of jewels.

"Sure," I told her, racing to get my phone first, just to make sure I had no new messages.

She snatched my phone away, and began using it. I realized that maybe she would understand and believe everything that Hunter had done. She has always looked up to me and believed me about everything. It seemed likely that she should be the one I tell. Even though I didn't trust her, not the slightest bit, I decided I would tell her a couple things.

"If I tell you a secret will you promise not to tell anyone?" I asked. She nodded and held out her pinky. Could she keep a secret? Would she think I was insane like my parents? I swallowed, and went for it.

"I've been receiving texts from Hunter lately."

"Hunter's dead. That's impossible; his phone was buried with him," she challenged.

"I know it sounds psycho, but it's true." Suddenly an idea came to me. "I have the texts on my phone! I can show you them right now!" I stole my phone from Catherine's tight grip and hurried to *Messages*. The messages were gone. I was so upset. My face became wet, and I just stared into her sparkling eyes.

"It's okay. I understand that you miss Hunter. Maybe your mind has been playing tricks on you, and you never actually received texts from him or read a new status of his on Facebook," Catherine replied, trying to sound helpful. I immediately realized that I hadn't told her anything about reading his Facebook status.

"What do you mean? I never told you I had seen his updated status on Facebook!" I stared at her in disbelief. How did she know that?

"You're losing your mind, you must have told me," she retorted. Suddenly my mind shook like an earthquake; I had no idea what to believe. Maybe I did tell her, but should I believe Hunter had been communicating with me? Or believe that I was mentally insane?

"I'm almost positive I never told you that, but it's not worth arguing about," I responded, doing my best to avoid starting an argument. After that, I told her I didn't feel well, which was just an excuse to get her to leave. As soon as she did, a familiar ringtone sounded in my ears.

"You left, without saying a word. And now, you're hidden from the world."

My heart immediately lunged out of my chest. My legs moved as quickly as a strong wind on a beach. I slid my phone open.

One new message from Hunter.

I don't think you are insane.

How had Hunter heard what Catherine and I had been talking about? Could he hear or see me right now? *BANG! BANG! BANG!* Startled by several knocks on the door, I threw my phone onto the kitchen counter. I sprinted to open up the door. Why was Catherine back? Ugh!

"Sorry to bother you, I had taken my bracelet off when you led me into your kitchen and I need it." She smiled apologetically, and then rushed into the kitchen. I sat on the couch waiting for her, and then when she returned with an ocean-foam-white bracelet, I told her to go fetch my phone. Once she did that, I knew I had proof.

"I received another text once you left!" I explained. I was excited to show her that I had been right all along. I could see a hint of fear in Catherine's emerald eyes—a fear that I was going crazy. No! I'm not! She'll see!

I slid my phone open and as quick as a hiccup, I was looking through my received texts. None from Hunter! Was I crazy?

"I really have to get going. Sorry!" She made her way out the door. I knew she was trying to avoid the fact that I was insane. I know I'm not insane though—don't I?

CHAPTER 3

DISCOVERING LIES

"Alicia, dinner time!" I could hear my mother call from the kitchen. I took a seat at the table. My plate of spaghetti noodles was flooded with tomato sauce and parmesan cheese. My mother sat down beside me; my father was working in his bedroom.

"So what did you and Catherine do?" my mother questioned, obviously trying to begin a conversation.

"Nothing really. Mom, I swear I received texts from Hunter!" My mom glanced at me, her chocolate-brown eyes looked sincere and sweet.

"It's okay. I understand that it's difficult when someone you were great friends with has passed away. I just think that maybe we should go to a counselor. People go to counselors all the time when people die; it's not strange. Maybe I can schedule an appointment for sometime tomorrow. You can tell them all about the texts and messages you have received; they will listen. I just want you to realize that Hunter is dead. He is not texting you—that would be impossible," my mom told me in a soft voice.

"Okay, fine. But he has been texting me! One day I will prove it to you!" I told her, getting a little bit carried away. I'm not crazy! Am I? My mom got up from the table, and started putting dishes away. Meanwhile, I went to the computer to get on Facebook. There was a new message from Hunter.

Everyone may think you're insane or crazy, but you're not. No matter who thinks that you're crazy, I never will!

My jaw dropped! I knew I wasn't crazy!

"MOM! COME QUICK!" I shouted from the living room, impatiently waiting for her. I watched her put the dish onto the kitchen counter and hurry to me.

"Are you okay?" she asked, looking as if she regretted coming over.

"Yeah! It's Hunter! He messaged me on Facebook." I twirled around so I was facing the computer—it was gone! Again! I couldn't believe it! I rubbed my eyes. I had no clue what to say. Maybe I was going insane. I watched my mother walk away; she seemed tired of hearing me tell her about all of these impossible events. A cold, salty river flowed down my face. I ran up the steps, escaping to my bedroom. Why did Hunter have to die? Was I going crazy? I could hear my mother from downstairs on the phone. She was scheduling an appointment with a counselor for tomorrow. Ugh!

"Alicia, come here!" my mother yelled, although it was barely audible from upstairs. I buried my face in my pillow; I just wanted to be alone. I peered over my shoulder to see my laptop sitting on the desk. It was so tempting to go onto

Facebook and search for any new messages, although I knew that if I received one, it would just vanish by the time I had a chance to show anyone. Everyone would just assume I was paranoid. The most difficult part about all of this was not knowing what to believe. Do I believe I'm psychotic, or do I believe I've been right all along, and that Hunter has been messaging me from Heaven?

"Alicia! Come down here please!" my mother begged from downstairs. I brought my hands to my face and wiped away any remaining tears. I dragged myself downstairs.

"What do you want?" I groaned, sinking down into the cream-colored couch cushions.

"Tomorrow at eleven o'clock you have an appointment with a counselor. Her name is Dr. Mary, and she is a great listener and very caring. I just talked with her on the phone, and she is very excited to meet you!" My mom smiled at me, clearly trying to make me feel more optimistic about the whole counselor situation. I just sat there and nodded.

"Honey, what exactly did those messages say? You know, the ones you received from Hunter?" she questioned, her eyes gleaming with curiosity.

"I don't know. They just said stuff like, 'It's so dark down here,' and that I'm not crazy, and that he missed everyone," I replied, once again gazing outside the window in the living room, trying to avoid her stare.

"Okay. That's all he said to you?" she wondered.

"Yeah," I said, getting up from the couch and going upstairs to prepare for bedtime. I was so tired, yet didn't want to fall asleep. The quicker I drifted to sleep, the quicker it would seem like time was passing, and I was not looking forward to eleven o'clock tomorrow. I began to put on my pajamas and brush my teeth, dreading the next day. I crept into my bed, pushing the covers to the side of me. It was too hot in my room. I peered outside the window like the night before, but the moon was too obscure to be seen. It hid behind many bold, damp grey clouds that surrounded the entire sky, blocking the view of any stars. Slowly, I drifted to sleep.

Before I knew it, I was awake. It was ten-thirty in the morning. I got dressed in a pink Aéropostale shirt and jeans, ate a bowl of cereal, and then rushed to the car to make it to the appointment on time. As my mother drove, we were both pretty silent. Once we arrived, we exited the car and entered a small building. We went to the room that Dr. Mary was in. She was gorgeous! She had glowing red hair down to her elbows, and her teeth were unusually white.

"Hello, you must be Alicia! It's a pleasure to meet you! Have a seat." She pointed to a chair across from her. My mom was standing in the doorway as Dr. Mary asked her if she could go into the waiting room. My mom left the room as quickly as a child could spend a dollar.

"So, your boyfriend Hunter died and you have been receiving texts and messages on Facebook from him?" Dr. Mary asked.

"Yes, I have. Everyone assumes I have gone psycho but I haven't! I saw real texts and messages from him! But as soon as I try to show someone them, they seem to disappear!" I explained.

"They do? What do these messages say?" she questioned. I told her all about what they said, word for word.

"How do you feel about receiving the messages? Are you excited he is texting you, or are you scared because you think you're going insane?" she asked.

"Well, at first I was excited, but after I realized that the evidence disappears, I became scared that I was imagining all of this," I admitted.

"Did he give his phone to anyone before he died?" she asked me, her eyes locked on mine.

"No. Everyone says it was buried with him."

"Okay. From now on whenever you see a text or message from him, I don't want you to open it. I want you to delete it. It would be healthier for you to not read these messages. Hunter is dead and it is not possible for him to be messaging you. So please, don't reply. Can you do this for me?" she asked, with her head slightly tilted.

I sighed. I nodded yes, and then she smiled at me.

"You're not insane. You just have a big imagination." Dr. Mary walked out of the room for a couple of minutes to talk with my mom.

What does she mean, "a big imagination"? I didn't imagine this! Although the truth is, I didn't even know if I would be able to delete messages from Hunter. It might not even be an option. I missed him. How did she expect me to delete something so valuable? Hunter was dead; what if the next message I was going to receive would be the last he would ever write to me? If I just deleted it, I would be paranoid it was something important. Those messages were so meaningful to me, even if I was just imagining them.

Click! Click! Click! I could hear the sounds of Dr. Mary's white heels knocking onto the shining auburn-colored floors. My mother and the counselor stepped into the cramped room.

"Thank you so much for taking the time to work with us," my mother thankfully told Dr. Mary.

"No, thank you. It's been wonderful meeting the both of you. Remember what I told you Alicia. Have a great day you two!" she cheerfully responded. My mother then signaled for us to leave and I stepped outside of the room. We made our way out to the parking lot and into my mom's grey van. It felt like our van was on fire! It was burning hot! I could hear the beeping of my mother's car keys turning on the car, and suddenly a cool breeze of air conditioning blew towards me.

"How did it go chatting with the counselor? She seemed very kind."

"Fine I guess. She said I had a big imagination. I didn't imagine this!" I returned. My mother didn't reply; she just continued driving. I began to realize how unlikely it would be that Hunter had been communicating with me. He was dead. He was never coming back, and maybe I hadn't yet become aware that my mind was reacting crazily to all of this. The reality of the situation had just punched me in the face. He wasn't messaging me. I was insane. I did have a big imagination. I felt like I was at war and had just surrendered—accepting defeat. I had believed with all of my heart that he was still talking to me through his cell phone. Now I came to the conclusion that all of that was fake. Maybe I was psycho. Maybe everyone had been right. I should have listened.

The car came to a halt. We were back at home. It was around one o'clock. Sunshine glared down all around our house. I felt my pocket vibrating, and as soon as my mother had shut the door to our house, I heard a familiar song play. Even though my feet burned, I stood as still as a child playing freeze tag.

"You left, without saying a word. And now, you're hidden from the world."

Oh no! I was paralyzed from shock. I'm just imagining this, right? Suddenly, my mind traveled backwards in time. I had a flashback to science class, my homeroom last Friday. I remembered that my teacher had heard the ringtone too! He had gotten onto me about it! I felt rescued, saved! Although, if he heard it, how come as soon as I read the message it disappeared? I felt like a detective, hopelessly lost. Everyone thought I was insane—I even believed I was. But if I'm really insane, how come my ringtone for Hunter was audible to multiple people?

My mind shattered like a glass hitting the concrete; should I read the text? Reading the text would let the counselor and my mother down, but deleting the text would leave me on edge and curious about what it could have said. Then again, curiosity killed the cat. Ugh! I couldn't take it anymore. Maybe, I would read the text and then make sure it was deleted. This way, I wouldn't let myself down, and I would delete it just like Dr. Mary wished. I came to the conclusion that I would read it and then delete it. I slid my phone open, holding my breath. Then I clicked *View Messages*.

I miss you. Hope you're having a good time. Don't worry about me. I'm doing great.

I hadn't really been worrying much about him. His second text to me had reassured me he was doing fine. I had just been so wrapped up in deciding whether I was crazy or not. After remembering that everyone in my science class had heard the audible ringtone too, I just didn't know what to think. I quickly deleted the message. I was wishing, praying that I wouldn't receive anymore. I was so confused; I felt like I had been on top of the world, and now like Hunter and his dad, I had come crashing down. Once again I tried asking myself if I was insane. But I still wasn't even close to finding an answer.

Almost instantly after that, I stopped staring at my phone and began running inside. My feet burned! I was completely unaware of how painfully hot the driveway had been! It had been so cold the last couple mornings, but today was the first day of spring and the weather seemed to warm up to one hundred degrees! I flung the door open and headed to the couch. I was tired, but not sleepy-tired. I was tired of being confused. I had no clue what to think about the situation I was in. It was so surreal. I felt like it was all a dream, except every time I tried pinching myself, I didn't wake up.

I could smell Ramen noodles cooking in the kitchen. I could also smell peanut butter and jelly. I pictured it being smothered together onto pieces of bread. I heard the milk being poured. My stomach felt empty, like I hadn't eaten in days—I was so ready for lunch.

Knock! Knock! I went to answer the door. My heart sank in my chest when I saw Catherine. The door began to creak open as I twisted the doorknob.

"Hey! Want to hang out today?" she asked, sounding like her usual peppy, vivacious, annoying self.

"I don't think I—" I started. My mom cut me off.

"She hasn't eaten lunch yet has she? Why doesn't she eat lunch over here, I'm fine with that," my mom said. Why couldn't my mother understand I didn't like her?

"I haven't eaten lunch yet! Sounds great—I would love to eat lunch over here! Thanks!" she reacted, smiling. She walked into my house, and we made our way to the kitchen.

I began eating silently, listening to Catherine tell me the most boring stories, like always. I saw her stuff her iPod and phone into her Vera Bradley bag. My mom went to her bedroom as we continued lunch.

"So, has Hunter said anything else to you lately?" she questioned, smirking.

"No, he hasn't," I lied, making sure I sounded as sane as possible.

"He must have, why would he just stop texting you?" she said, her hands moving her bangs behind her ears and away from her tan-looking face.

"Can we just talk about something else?" I managed to respond.

"I guess, but nothing is as interesting," she laughed. She began talking about how her parents may agree to her getting a hamster for her birthday, and I zoned out. My head, which was lying on the kitchen table, shot up like a rocket when I heard a familiar song play. Catherine must have heard it this time!

"You left, without saying a word. And now, you're hidden from the world. But I, still remember, the last day in December, when there was still a you and me, everything, fit together perfectly."

I couldn't believe what I had heard! Was it my phone? Whenever I received messages from Hunter the ringtone never played nearly as much of the song! And my phone was on the other side of the kitchen—the sound seemed like it had played all around me! I darted across the kitchen and slid my phone open. No new messages.

"What are you doing?" Catherine wondered, staring at me.

"You didn't hear that? That music play?" I asked, stunned! I was so agitated that no one else heard it!

"No. What did it sound like?" she asked.

"Nothing. It doesn't really matter," I responded on the edge of crying. How come I was the only one who heard this? Why did you have to die Hunter? I would have been so much better off if he was still alive. No one would think I was crazy. I made my way back to the kitchen table. Catherine was just looking at me.

"I have to go somewhere at two, so you better get going." I lied, although I'm not sure if she fell for it or not.

"Okay. Well, bye. See you at school tomorrow!" She left, getting her shoes from my front porch. As soon as she shot out the door, I figured out she had left her Vera Bradley. I felt lazy and instead of walking over to my cell phone, I decided that I would just use hers to call her house. I opened her bag. Suddenly, I could care less about having to call her—I found her iPod. It was paused on the song "Wordless Goodbye." She had been the one to play it! And the fact that she had paused it meant that she had purposely played it! But why? Did she even have any clue that it was my ringtone for Hunter? I couldn't think of one good reason she would play that song and then deny hearing anything. Why would she do that?

I grabbed Catherine's phone and called her house. It rang a couple of times, then Catherine picked up.

"Hey Catherine, it's Alicia. You left your phone at my house, along with your Vera Bradley. We need to talk."

"Oh okay! Thanks for calling me! And talk about what?" Her voice sounded shaky.

"Why was your iPod paused on the song "Wordless Goodbye"? That's exactly the song I had heard playing in the kitchen. Why did you deny hearing it if you're the one who played it?" I asked, demanding an answer.

"What do you mean? I had been listening to it at my house. I never played or heard it in your kitchen. Why would I do something like that?" Her voice sounded a little bit angry with me for thinking she would do that.

"Oh. Sorry then. I'll bring your Vera Bradley to school tomorrow. Bye," I said, hanging up shortly after.

Why had she lied? It was obvious she had lied. Her iPod was paused exactly at the part of the song that was no longer audible in the kitchen. What was she trying to do? Maybe she was just trying to help me understand that I was going a little bit crazy ever since I told her that I had gotten texts from Hunter. Maybe, she was just trying to help me realize that my mind was playing tricks on me and that the texts were not real. But still—why would anyone do something like that? The part that agitated me was that even on the phone she refused to admit it! How stubborn of her! I had never liked that girl, and now I disliked her a whole lot more!

I became bored, and went up to my bedroom, just to think. I had been doing a lot of thinking lately, and I still had no clue what was happening. I had no grip on the situation and couldn't solve any of my problems. I went onto Facebook out of boredom. I had a message, as usual. I didn't want to read it, but it was so tempting. Before I knew it my eyes were moving left to right.

You're not crazy! You can actually see this message can't you? Believe me, you're sane. And forgiving and forgetting heals life's problems.

I wished I could trust this message. But I knew it wasn't real. Soon it would vanish. The only place I would ever be able to find this message again would be my memory. And what does Hunter mean by forgive and forget? Forgive Catherine for lying to me and making me believe I was even crazier? No. That would be difficult to do. Not until she apologized for being a liar.

I ate a late dinner, and then went to bed. I had a nightmare, a nightmare that I was really psychotic! Catherine had told everyone in school my situation and they all thought I was insane. My friend Jenny never wanted to talk to me again. It was the worst dream I had ever had. That was my fear—everyone would find out that I was going crazy!

CHAPTER 4

GOLD WITH BLACK CALLIGRAPHY

Beep! Beep! Beep! I pulled my hand over and slammed the alarm off. I yanked myself out of bed to prepare for school. After I was ready and dressed in my ruffled white skirt and navy blue shirt, I headed for the bus stop. The weather outside was warm. The clouds overhead threatened rain. I saw Catherine waiting at the top of the hill. She had a smile on her face like usual, acting as if nothing was wrong. I returned her handbag, and then waited for the bus.

"You seem so quiet today. What's wrong?" Catherine demanded. As if she didn't know!

"Why did you lie?" I begged.

"I didn't. It must have been a coincidence. I'm sorry if it seemed that way." She sounded so sincere, but I knew better than to believe her. Even though I knew she was lying, I remembered Hunter's advice to forgive and forget.

"It's fine," I whispered. An enormous gust of wind blew in my face as the bus dashed around the corner and came to an immediate halt. I grabbed the seat by the window—like usual.

"I called your house yesterday, your mom told me that you were in your room and so I asked if you could come over after school today. She said it was fine, and to call her once you got to my house! Aren't you excited?" she asked, practically bouncing up and down in the bus seat.

"Well, I guess, but don't you come to my house every day anyway?"

"Yeah!" she vivaciously replied. Her emerald eyes seemed to light up whenever she was optimistic. I banged into the seat in front of me as the bus stopped in the school parking lot. As we exited the bus, I gathered everything I needed and made my way to my science class. Before class started, I turned to the coffee-brown-haired boy who sat next to me.

"So on Friday do you remember when my phone went off?" I asked, double-checking he had heard the ringtone too.

"Yeah," he mumbled, looking at me like I was a stranger.

"You heard it go off, right?" He nodded! He did hear it go off! I knew he did, but that reassurance gave me new hope! I had felt like I was in the bottom of a deep abyss, but now I was climbing my way to the top. I felt more likely to be sane now! I for sure wasn't the only person who had heard my ringtone go off, and that was a huge relief. Whew! I sighed, smiling.

Time passed, and during class I zoned out, imagining ways to prove to my mother and Dr. Mary that they had been wrong all along. The only thing I couldn't figure out was why the messages were disappearing!

Rrrrrriiiiinnnnnnggggg! The final bell sounded. Hundreds of kids poured out of their classrooms like angry bees exiting their nests. I spotted Catherine in the crowd and we boarded our bus once again, finally able to put schoolwork aside.

"Hey! So you're going to my house right after we are dropped off," she reminded me. Why did she keep telling me this? It's not like I could forget having to be around her almost 24/7! She would easily get on my last nerve. Oh well, it's not like I would be at her house more than a couple of hours, considering that I would have to go home for dinner anyway. Finally I heard the whoosh of the bus doors opening, and Catherine and I strolled down to her house.

Catherine opened up her door, and we entered her house. We darted up to her room, and then sat on her bed watching TV. Her walls were painted a charcoal grey with a lively light purple polka-dot print. Her bed was a light purple as well. She had a desk with a computer sitting on it to the left of us.

"I have to go to the bathroom. Be right back!" she explained, heading in the other direction. I became bored of watching TV and went to sit on the fuzzy purple chair in front of the desk. Bored, I opened up the desk drawer. My heart stopped. My breath came to a halt. I wanted to scream, but found that it wasn't possible. In the desk lay several photos of Hunter and me together, and a sheet of paper that had mine and

Hunter's Facebook usernames and passwords written on it. Also, a phone. The case was a shiny unforgettable gold, with black calligraphy letters spelling out "Hunter."

"What do you think you're doing?" her hushed voice asked in an eerie whisper; Catherine was directly behind me. I bit my bottom lip, held my breath, and turned around.

AFTERWORD

I haven't seen Catherine for several months now. Every morning when I make my way to the bus stop the only audible sound is the singing birds. I sit in my bus seat, alone. When we pass down her street I always glance at the "FOR SALE" sign sitting in her yard. She has been staying at her lake house about an hour away. She had been the one to start the rumor that Hunter was buried with his phone—obviously he wasn't. I can't imagine ever speaking with her again. Every day, things seem to be getting back to normal. I've even stopped seeing Dr. Mary. Everyone now knows that Catherine was the crazy one.

But why is it, then, that I'm still getting texts from Hunter?